ABC Nature Riddles

by Susan Joyce

illustrations by

Doug DuBosque

Peel Productions, Inc.

Published by Peel Productions, Inc.
PO Box 546, Columbus NC 28722
http://peelbooks.com

Printed in Hong Kong

For Lauren and Michael

L_____y of Congress

Cataloging-in-publication data

Joyce, Susan, 1945–
ABC nature riddles / by Susan Joyce ;
illustrations by Doug DuBosque
p. cm.

Summary: Rhyming alphabet-based riddles challenge the reader to identify aspects of nature from clues, including the first and last letter of the word.

ISBN 0-939217-53-8 (alk. paper)

1. Riddles, Juvenile. 2. Nature Juvenile literature 3. English language--Alphabet juvenile literature [1. Riddles. 2. Nature. 3. Alphabet.] I. DuBosque, D. C., ill. II. Title.

PN6371.5.J678 1999
508--dc21 99-21343

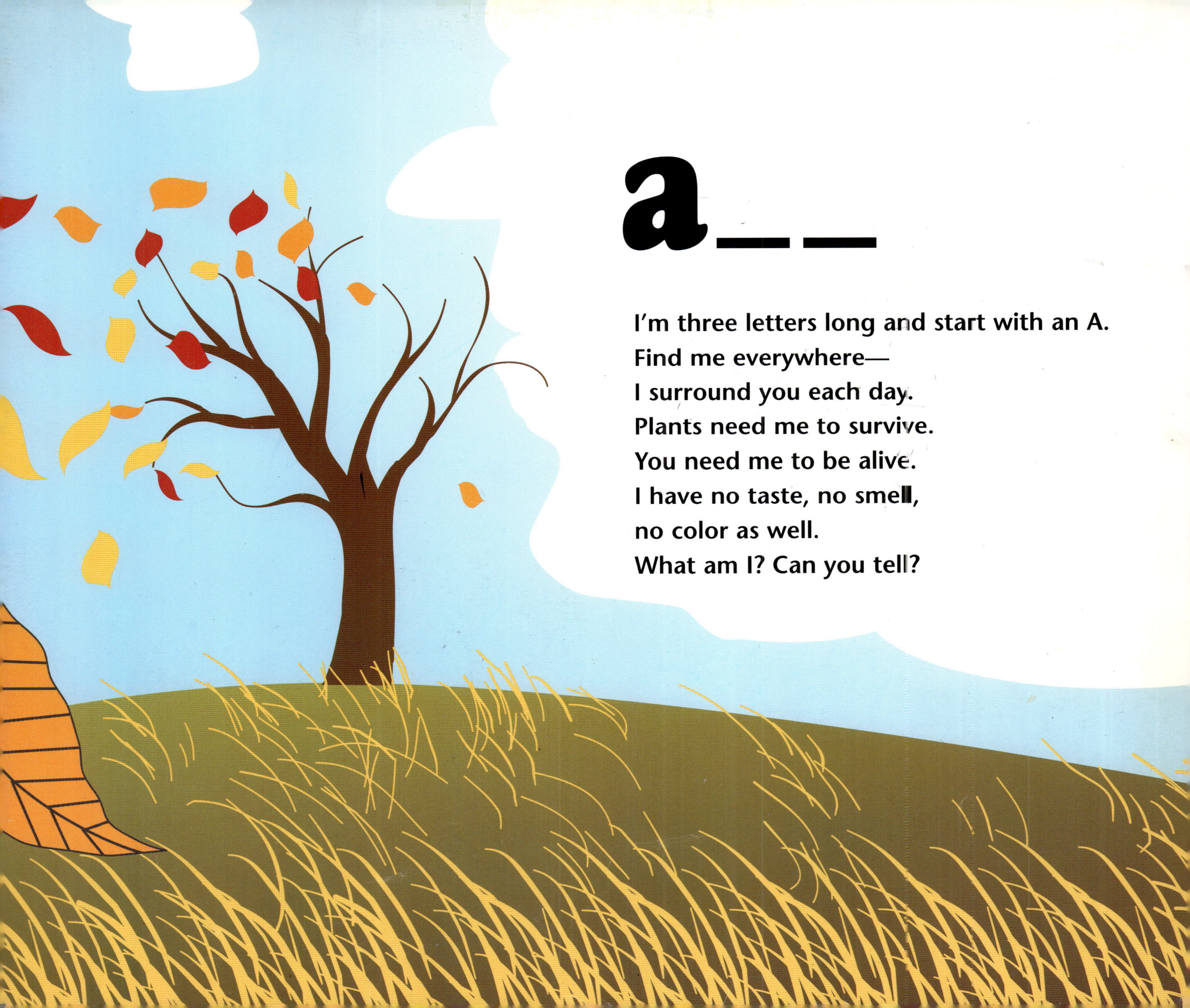

a_ _

I'm three letters long and start with an A.
Find me everywhere—
I surround you each day.
Plants need me to survive.
You need me to be alive.
I have no taste, no smell,
no color as well.
What am I? Can you tell?

b___

I'm four letters long and start with a B.
A warm-blooded creature,
you like to watch me.
I have slender legs
and lay hard-shelled eggs.
My call is unique
and so is my beak.
I walk, swim or fly.
Can you guess? What am I?

c___d

I start with a C and end with a D.
When I am new,
I'm white and fluffy.
My shape and size change
when I rearrange.
I bring rain. I bring snow.
What am I? Do you know?

d _ _ _ _ t

I start with a D and end with a T.
I'm a place where there's sun,
but seldom a tree.
I'm a dry barren land
with dunes of fine sand—
where dust dances 'round
and makes a *whoosh* sound,
where tumbleweeds fly
and stars beam from the sky
Can you guess? What am I?

e _ _ _ _

I'm five letters long and start with an E.
Between Venus and Mars,
I spin steadily.
With each of my spins
a new day begins.
Plants and animals live on me.
What's my name? What can I be?

f___

I start with an F. I'm four letters long.
I can be small,
or quite big and strong.
I can be flat
or be round and fat.
Through the water I sail,
with my fins and a tail.
Sometimes I even fly.
Can you guess? What am I?

g _ _ _ _

I'm five letters long, I start with a G.
I grow in the fields—
all grains come from me.
I make food for you
and animals too.
I'm something you sow
and something you mow.
What am I? Do you know?

h _ _ _ _ _ _ _ e

I start with an H and end with an E.
A very big storm,
I begin in the sea.
My loud, howling wind
can make a tree bend,
or blow houses down
all over a town.
If you hear or see me,
seek shelter or flee.
What can I possibly be?

i _ _ _ _ t

I start with an I and end with a T.
An animal I am,
but I'm small as can be.
I have three pairs of legs
and lay hundreds of eggs.
My antennae help me feel
all around for a meal.
With wings, I can fly.
Can you guess? What am I?

j____e

I start with a J and end with an E.
I'm a warm, wet place
with a green canopy.
My floor is filled with plants,
lots of critters—bugs and ants....
You'll find snakes galore,
colorful birds and more.
I'm home to tall trees,
crocodiles and monkeys.
I'm an amazing place to see.
What can I be?

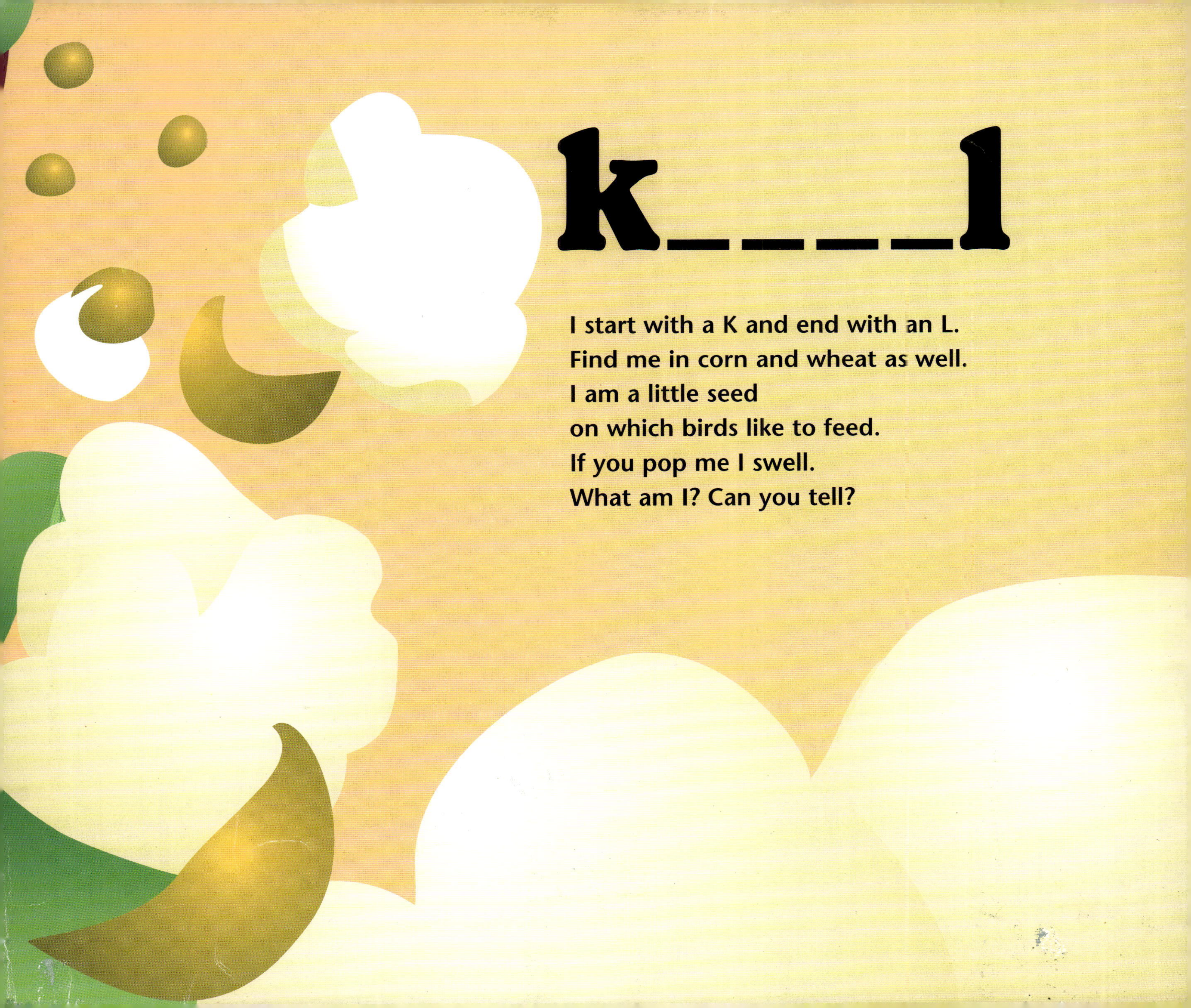

k _ _ _ _ l

I start with a K and end with an L.
Find me in corn and wheat as well.
I am a little seed
on which birds like to feed.
If you pop me I swell.
What am I? Can you tell?

l _ _ _

I'm four letters long and start with an L.
I'm a pool of fresh water
where schools of fish dwell.
I'm a place you like to go—
to swim, sail or row.
What am I? Do you know?

m___

I'm four letters long. I start with an M.
At times I am bright.
At times I am dim.
In space I am found
spinning around.
My light you can see
when the sun shines on me.
What can I be?

n_ _ _

I'm four letters long and start with an N.
Animals build me,
to lay their young in.
I'm made with a mix—
sometimes grass, sometimes sticks.
Find me in a tree
or in sand near the sea.
What am I? Can you name me?

O _ _

I'm three letters long. I start with an O.
I'm a liquid that helps
machines start and go.
You can use me for heat
and for cooking your meat.
From the ground I flow.
What am I? Do you know?

p_ _ _ _

I'm five letters long
and I start with a P.
I can be very small
or be large like a tree.
With water and air,
I can live anywhere.
I need sunlight to grow.
What am I? Do you know?

q___e

I start with a Q and end with an E.
With no advance warning,
I move land and sea.
My waves ripple out
and shake things about.
It's a very wild ride—
up and down, side to side.
Big buildings will sway
if they stand in my way.
What am I? Can you say?

r_ _ _ _

I'm five letters long
and I start with an R.
I run from the top,
and I run quite far.
My banks have mud and goo,
and water snakes too.
I'm always in motion,
as I head for the ocean,
or a lake near by.
Can you guess? What am I?

S___

I'm four letters long,
I start with an S.
I'm a big ball of fire,
filled with very hot gas.
A fixed point of light,
I shine every night
I'm far, far away.
What am I? Can you say?

t______

I'm seven letters long and start with a T.
When I roar and rumble,
I'm loud as can be.
Air heated by lightning—
My sound is quite frightening.
First you'll see a flash,
then you'll hear a crash,
if a storm's not far away.
What am I? Can you say?

u______e

I start with a U and end with an E.
You can only see a small part of me.
I'm the sun, moon and stars,
Venus, Jupiter and Mars.
I'm big and I'm wide,
I'm all that's outside.
I'm all things that be.
Can you name me?

v_ _ _ _y

I start with a V and end with a Y.
Find me between
the mountain peaks high.
I'm the flat land below,
where a river may flow
and where vegetables grow.
What am I? Do you know?

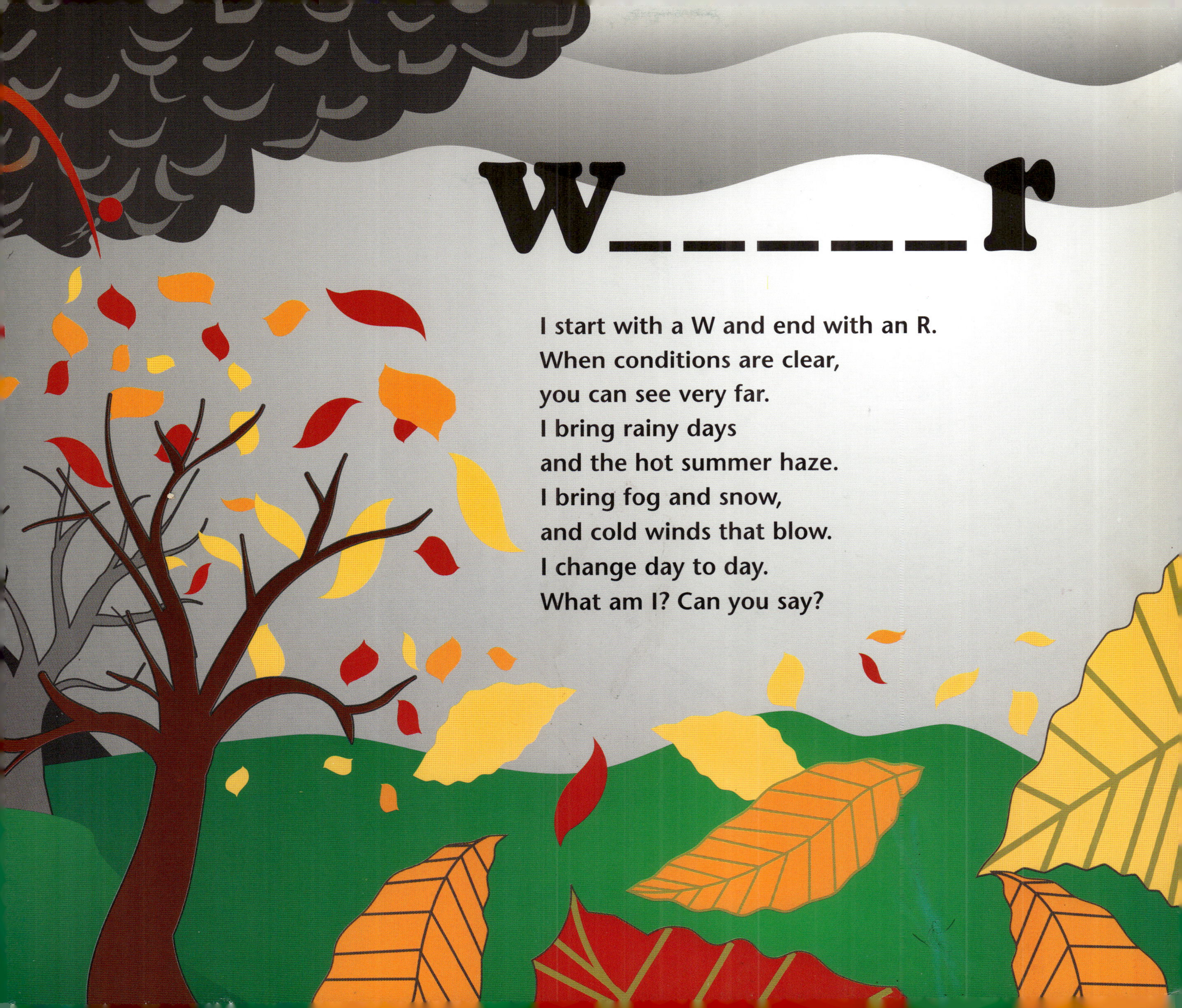

W_____r

I start with a W and end with an R.
When conditions are clear,
you can see very far.
I bring rainy days
and the hot summer haze.
I bring fog and snow,
and cold winds that blow.
I change day to day.
What am I? Can you say?

_ X _ _ _ _ _

X is the second letter in my name.
There are six more letters,
two are the same.
I'm something you do
to learn something new—
when you scout and look about
or read to find things out.
I am the key
to a great discovery.
I'm fun and often free.
Can you name me?

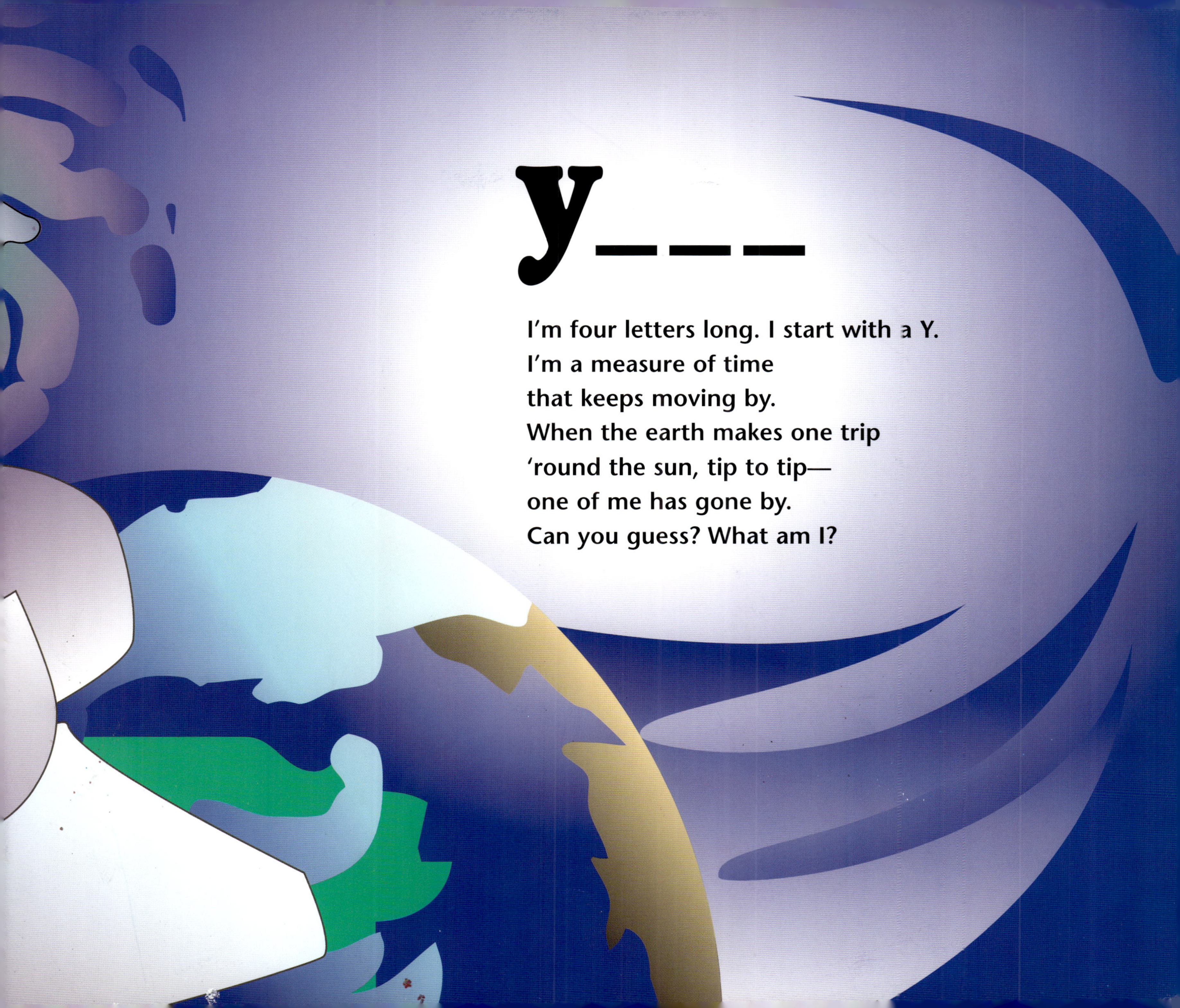

y___

I'm four letters long. I start with a Y.
I'm a measure of time
that keeps moving by.
When the earth makes one trip
'round the sun, tip to tip—
one of me has gone by.
Can you guess? What am I?

_ Z _ _ _

My name has five letters, the second is Z.
I'm a blue gas formed by electricity.
I'm important indeed—
something you always need.
I block the sun's rays,
that cause harm in many ways.
My shield is thinner than it used to be.
What am I? Can you name me?

air
bird
cloud
desert
earth
fish
grass
hurricane
insect
jungle
kernel
lake
moon
nest
oil
plant
quake
rainbow
star
thunder
universe
valley
weather
explore
year
ozone

Ideas for Parents and Teachers

As a young child, I had dyslexia and had a very difficult time reading, writing and speaking words. Fortunately, my parents believed that children can learn language and be entertained at the same time. So as a family we played a word game we called alphabet riddles. We would invent riddles while riding in the car, or waiting on a bus, or whenever we had a few minutes to spare. It worked like magic. It made learning words fun!

Creating nature riddles that rhyme is a wonderful way to explore words. As you engage children personally in the poetic process, you will see them blossom in their vocabulary, their understanding of words and their meanings. You will help them develop reading, writing, thinking and vocal presentation skills.

~ Create nature riddles! They don't have to be fancy. Choose something in nature you like. Think of words that describe the object. Begin the riddle with letter and word clues. Start with a simple riddle:

I start with an S and end with a Y.
Find me outside when you look way up high.

~ Stretch the exercise. Look up the definition of the word in the dictionary. Read the definition aloud. Add more lines with more clues to the riddle. End the riddle with a question inviting an answer.

When the sun shines through
I'm beautifully blue.
I'm not the sea.
What can I be?

~ Share riddles! Written riddles can be solved independently, but it's always more fun to share a rhyming riddle. So, write it down and then share it with others.

~ In a group, instruct children to wait until all clues have been given before guessing the riddle. Allow the first child who guesses the answer to say the correct word, spell it, or write it on the blackboard. Then, the child may create a new nature riddle or choose someone else to make up one.

~ Encourage children, as an extended activity, to draw the nature object.

Enjoy!

Susan Joyce

n _ _ _ _ e

I start with an N and end with an E.
I'm all that you see,
not made by you or me—
the moon in the sky,
the clouds floating by,
the monkey and the tree,
the mountain and the sea.
I'm also you and me.
What can I possibly be?

DATE			